Frank
and the
Masked Cat

Martha Brockenbrough

illustrated by Jon Lau

LQ
LEVINE QUERIDO

MONTCLAIR · AMSTERDAM · HOBOKEN

This is an Arthur A. Levine book
Published by Levine Querido

www.levinequerido.com · info@levinequerido.com
Levine Querido is distributed by Chronicle Books, LLC
Text copyright © 2023 by Martha Brockenbrough
Illustrations copyright © 2023 by Jon Lau
All rights reserved
Library of Congress Cataloging-in-Publication data is available
ISBN 978-1-64614-242-2
Printed and bound in China

Published in March 2023
First Printing
The text type was set in Perpetua Regular
Jon Lau created the illustrations for
this picture book by painting the characters, objects,
and backgrounds using poster color paints on sheets
of BFK Rives printmaking paper.
He then scanned the paintings and assembled the illustrations
in Adobe Photoshop, much like a digital collage.

To Adam, my own true raccoon
                    —M.B.

CHAPTER 1

Sunny in the Dark

Sunny's body had the ya-yas.

She had them all the way from her snoot to her tail.

"Yikes," the humans said. "Time for your walk."

Frank's mind also had the ya-yas.

But he could not take his mind on a walk.

His mind was stuck in his head, his head was stuck on his body, and he was stuck in his house.

His mind zoomed with questions.

Where is Sunny?

That was the biggest one. All the
rest were about Cap'n Keith.
He was the rude parrot who'd come
to stay for a while.

How bad must
he be to live his
life in a cage on
wheels?

Was he a
bank robber?

A mad bomber?

Someone who splooped
on heads?

"He'll only be here for a short while," Frank's humans had said.

"Ha," Frank said.

"HA."

"HA," Cap'n Keith said. "Squawk."

Frank puffed his fur and pressed his nose to the window.

Where was Sunny?

Cap'n Keith cracked seeds in his beak. He spit shells on the floor.

"Quiet," Frank said.

"Quiet," Cap'n Keith said. Then he laughed.

That did it! Frank swiped at Cap'n Keith.

He missed, but it was on purpose.

"Bilge rat!" Cap'n Keith said. "Bilge rat!"

Frank hissed. He was not a rat.

He was not bilge—whatever that was.

"I bet you taste like chicken,"
Frank said.

"Squawk," Cap'n Keith said. "Do not."

Frank blinked back tears. What if Sunny was lost forever?

He looked outside again and a shrub wiggled.

Sunny?

"Naw," Cap'n Keith said.

Cap'n Keith was right.

This was not Sunny.

CHAPTER TWO

The Magnificent Masked Cat

In a puddle of moonlight stood a magnificent cat.

She had nifty black paws.

A long tail with splendid rings.

A mask to hide her identity.

She was an enigma, which is an extra-beautiful mystery.

Frank could not move.

"Squawk," Cap'n Keith said. "Swoon."

The masked cat strolled to the carport. She stood on her back paws. She slid the lid off the trash can.

Clang!

Went the lid.

Clang!

Went Frank's heart.

The magnificent, masked cat leaned into the trash. She plucked out an apple core. She held it in her nifty paws. She nibbled it.

Who was she, behind that mask?

Why was she nibbling an apple core from the trash?

How did his belly get so full of ya-yas?

Cap'n Keith flapped and
stamped. "Squawk. True love. You're
doomed."

Then something outside went
bappity-bap.

Sunny was home!

This was the good news.

The bad news was, she'd chased away Frank's one true love.

Sunny zoomed inside and licked Frank's face.

"I spooked a bandit," she said.
"Did I make you proud?"

Frank wiped his face with his
favorite paw.

"Yes," he said. "So proud."

He had to say this. He did not want to make Sunny sad.

Frank sighed and fetched his diary.

CHAPTER THREE

It's Private

"Dear Diary," he wrote.

Frank felt hot breath on his neck.

"Sunny," he said.

"Are we writing a strongly worded letter?" Sunny asked.

"No," Frank said.

"Is it a poem? I wrote this one for
you.

"*Roses are red.*

"*Whiskies are brown.*

"*Your name is Frank and mine is*
Sunny."

"That doesn't rhyme," Frank said.

"I can't do that part yet," Sunny said.

"Sunny," he said. "Go get ready for bed."

Frank picked up his pen.

"I am brushing my teeth!" Sunny called out. "I have washed my face! And my hiney!"

Frank stopped writing.

Sunny zoomed back with a crayon and a book.

"Are we writing bucket lists?" she asked.

"We already did bucket lists," Frank said. "Go put on your jammies."

"I will sleep nude," Sunny said. "Like you. That's the only thing on my bucket list. Be like Frank."

Frank closed his diary and locked it. He gave Sunny a look.

Sunny put her head on her paws. "You are so grumpy, Frank. What is wrong?"

"NOTHING IS WRONG," Frank said. "NOTHING."

"Frank's in love," Cap'n Keith said. "Squawk."

Sunny made a face. "How can he get out of it?"

"No way out," Cap'n Keith said. "Love is a cage. A cage you can't see."

"We must rescue Frank," Sunny said. "We MUST."

CHAPTER 4

The Love Dance

"If love is a cage," Frank said, "then I am its prisoner."

"Wow, Frank," Sunny said. "That was a poem that did not rhyme."

"No poems!" Cap'n Keith said. "Frank needs the love dance."

"What's that?" Sunny asked.

"Let me out and I'll show you," Cap'n Keith said.

"Don't do it, Sunny," Frank said. "Cap'n Keith is a criminal."

"Is that true?" Sunny said. "Are you a criminal, Cap'n Keith?"

"I'm innocent,"

Cap'n Keith said. Then he whistled.

"All right then," Sunny
said. "I will set you free."

She put her paws on the cage.
"Whoops."

The cage slid all the way across
the room.

Bonk!

It crashed against the bookshelf.

"Squawk!" Cap'n Keith said.

"Oh no," Sunny said.

Frank got on the bookshelf so he could take a look. He did not care for Cap'n Keith. But he didn't want him to be hurt.

One of the humans rushed in.

"What's going on in here?" he asked. He scooped up Frank. "If you

can't leave that bird alone, I'll put you in your carrier."

Cap'n Keith whistled.

Then the human scratched Sunny behind her ears. "Good puppy. Good puppy." Then he left.

Sunny said, "I'm glad you didn't

get put in your carrier, Frank. It is bad enough that you are a prisoner of love."

"Hey, Frank," Cap'n Keith said, "wanna learn a Love Dance?" He moved his head and wings in a weird way.

"That is not for me," Frank said.

"LOOK AT ME!" Sunny said.

"I am Love Dancing! Whoops!"

Sunny did not Love Dance for long.
It is not easy to stand on two back legs.
Not unless you are Frank or his masked
love. Then you are an expert.

"Squawk," Cap'n Keith said.

It was a soft squawk, soft and sad.

Frank stroked his handsome chin.

He felt a pang. Poor Cap'n Keith.

No one—not a heart, and not
even a loud parrot—belongs in a cage.

CHAPTER 5

The Love Letter

Late that night, Frank paced the room. The moon was high. Even the owls had gone to bed.

His heart was a bottle, stopped up with feelings. He did not know how to pour them out.

At last, Frank got an idea. He
fetched his keyboard.

"My dearest," he wrote, for he did
not know her name.

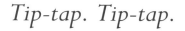

Tip-tap. Tip-tap.

Tip-tap. Tip-tap.

The sound was like

branches in a windstorm.

Like Whiskies into a

bowl. Like a poem that

did not rhyme.

Tip-tap. Tip-tap.

The sound was like his

heart.

He wrote all through the night.

The next day, Frank woke up late.
The sun was in his face.

So was Sunny. Her breath smelled
like Puppy Grub.

"Frank!" she said. "Your letter is great!"

"Sunny," Frank said, "you should not have read that. It was *private*."

"I am sorry, Frank. I did not know that love letters are private."

"It is all right, Sunny. Just do not do it again, please."

"No problem," Sunny said. "I already read it five times. I know it by heart. But I have a question."

"Yes, Sunny?"

"If the letter is private, how will your darling Poopsie with the niftyhands and mysterious mask know what it says?"

"Sunny!"

"Yes, Frank?"

"That was the rough draft. I crossed out Poopsie in the final copy."

"Oh," Sunny said. "May I read the final copy?"

"No!" Frank said.
"It is private between
the cat and me. *She* is
allowed to read it."

"But I thought privacy
was what you had *alone*, Frank.
That's what you always tell me."

"Things can be private between
two souls," Frank said.

"That is great news for my
bucket list," Sunny said.

"Ha-ha," Cap'n Keith said.
"Squawk."

"Cap'n Keith and I have a surprise," Sunny said. "We made you a gondola!"

"Squawk," Cap'n Keith said. "It's a boat for lovers."

Sunny dragged a box into the room. It was Frank's lair. But Sunny had decorated it.

"Get in!" Sunny said.

Frank got in. He felt silly but he did not want to make Sunny sad.

"Sing a song," she said. "A song of love."

"No, thank you," Frank said.

"I will," Cap'n Keith said.

"Oh, solay meow."

Is he trying to speak cat?

Frank thought.

"Throw the birdseed, Frank," Sunny said. "It is a romantic thing to do."

Frank tried. He had never been good at sports.

"Squawk," Cap'n Keith said.

"What now?" Sunny said.

"We play the waiting game,"
Frank said. He was good at that.

Sunny rolled on her back. "This is
not a fun game, Frank."

"Squawk!" Cap'n Keith said. "More fun than a cage."

When the sun went down, Frank pressed his nose against the glass.

Where was that magnificent cat?

What if she didn't come back?

How could he survive?

At last, the shrub rustled.

"Frank!" Sunny said.

"I know," he said.

He booped her nose. The time
had come. Sunny shoved his gondola
into the darkness.

And then Frank uncaged his
heart.

CHAPTER 7

The Delivery

Up close, the cat was more magnificent than Frank had imagined.

She was at least twice his size.

Her eyes were wondrous. They were two silver saucers. Priceless pearls. A pair of moons.

"Shoot," Frank thought. "I should have put that in the letter. Oh well. I will put it in the next one."

He would write nine lifetimes of love letters.

The cat rose on her hind legs.

He did, too.

He tossed birdseed into the night
sky and lay the letter at her feet.
"For you," he purred.

The cat took the letter in her nifty paws.

She had long, elegant fingers, almost like a human's.

"Wow," he said.

He gazed into her eyes, her
saucers, her pearls, her moons.

She smiled and made a noise that
sounded like the paper of a rough
draft being torn in two: *Hissssssssss*.

She unfolded the letter. She used
her nifty paws to tear it into shreds.
Then she stuffed them in her mouth.

She swallowed it.

Then she picked up
the seeds and ate
them.

"Oh solay meow," Frank sang.
He even he did the dance. "Step into
my gondola, my Poopsie."

The masked cat stopped chewing.

She lowered herself to all four
paws.

Then she moved, like a poem
that rhymed, into the night.

CHAPTER 8

True Love

"Are you all right, Frank?" Sunny asked. "Are you still in love with that cat who I am pretty sure is a criminal even though she is not in a cage?"

"I am, Sunny," Frank said. "I am. The heart has no use for the law."

"She ate your letter, Frank."

"That's because she loved it so much," Frank said.

"Wow, Frank. I am sure you are right. You know everything about love there is to know."

"It's true," Frank said. "I also know about something else."

He whispered to Sunny.

70

"Great idea," she said.

She stood beneath Cap'n Keith's cage. Frank stood on her back, balancing on his hind legs. He reached for the latch.

"Squawk?" Cap'n Keith said, as softly as any parrot could. Frank did not have fingers like his lady love, but his paws were nimble. He moved them up and down. Side to side. Like a love dance.

"Click!" the cage swung open.

"Squawk!" The parrot stepped
into Frank's arms. Whoa. Cap'n
Keith was heavy.

Frank wobbled. Then Sunny
wobbled.

"SQUAWK!"
Cap'n Keith said.

"Yikes," Frank said.

"Whoa," Sunny said.

Frank and Sunny fell into a heap.

Cap'n Keith landed on top of them.

He smelled like chicken.

"I love chicken," Frank said.

"Do not eat me," Cap'n Keith said.

"Frank would never," Sunny said.

"I promise," Frank said.

"Just in case," Cap'n Keith said.

He flew back into his cage.

Frank's mind was full. A cage was a prison. But it could also keep you safe.

You could not like a parrot very much. And then you could love him. Not the way you loved Sunny. Not the way you loved the masked cat.

But the way you loved someone
whose heart you understood.

"Love is pretty weird, Frank,"
Sunny said.

"You're right, Sunny," he said.

Love was the weirdest. But it was also wonderful.

He put his paws around Sunny and licked her head the way she liked.

"Love you, Sunny," Cap'n Keith said. "Love you, Frank. Squawk! Good night!"